TALL TAILS
CROSS-COUNTRY WITH LEWIS AND CLARK

D0167958

ENJOY ALL OF THE BOOKS IN THE
TALL TAILS SERIES:

TALL TAILS #1
Wingin' It with the Wright Brothers

TALL TAILS #2
Cross-Country with Lewis and Clark

TALL TAILS

Cross-Country with
LEWIS AND CLARK

BY DONA SMITH

ILLUSTRATIONS BY
GUY FRANCIS

A
LITTLE APPLE
PAPERBACK

SCHOLASTIC INC.
New York   Toronto   London   Auckland   Sydney
Mexico City   New Delhi   Hong Kong   Buenos Aires

For Joy and Aimee,
with many thanks.

ISBN 0-439-43441-6

Text copyright © 2004 by Dona Smith.
Illustrations copyright © 2004 by Scholastic Inc.
All rights reserved. Published by Scholastic Inc. SCHOLASTIC, LITTLE APPLE, and associated logos are trademarks and/or registered trademarks of Scholastic Inc.

Design by Joyce White

12 11 10 9 8 7 6 5 4 3 2   4 5 6 7 8 9/0

Printed in the U.S.A.   40
First printing, May 2004

Dear Reader,

I have learned to believe the unbelievable. Read on, and you will, too.

It all started the day I brought my terrier puppy, Elvis, home. Elvis was different from any other dog I had known. For one thing, he loved to read. Strange as it sounds, I often found him curled up with a book.

Then one day Elvis wrote me a note. I wouldn't have believed it if I hadn't seen it with my own eyes. Here is what he wrote:

Dear Dona,

Please follow me to the park. It is time for you to know the truth.

Elvis

Of course I followed him. What else could I do? When we got to the park, Elvis began to dig and dig. Soon, he uncovered an old wooden trunk with a bone carved on the front.

Inside the trunk I found several dog-eared

volumes. Each was a diary telling about history from a dog's point of view. I read them and discovered that dogs played a role in many of history's golden moments and great inventions. I showed them to my editors, Joy Peskin and Aimee Friedman. We decided that we must publish these diaries. Now it is time for you, too, to know the truth.

In *this* diary, which tells the story of the Lewis and Clark expedition, Elvis added a few notes at the start of — and throughout — the chapters to explain key locations visited by the Corps of Discovery. Elvis also added the location at the start of each diary entry. Much of the United States territory had not been named at the time of Lewis and Clark. These notes will help you keep track of their progress. Enjoy the trip!

Best wishes,
Dona Smith
Joy Peskin
Aimee Friedman
Elvis

CHAPTER 1
July 9–
September 20, 1803

You never know where life will take you. Seaman always wanted to stay put on the Pittsburgh, Pennsylvania wharves with his family and friends. To him, swimming, eating, and sleeping made up the perfect dog's life. Then, one day, he found himself getting ready for an incredible adventure. He had a chance to journey into unknown territory and go down in history as a famous hero.

It was the last thing he wanted.

July 9, 1803

The Pittsburgh wharves

My name is Seaman. I am a pretty unusual dog. I can do things most other dogs can't, like see in color. Most dogs are pretty good swimmers, but I take to water like a fish! I'm a Newfoundland — a water dog — and I even have webbed feet, like a duck.

People might also think I am unusual because I can read and write. Ruff-ruff! Shows what *they* know. *All* dogs can read and write. We have to keep it a secret, though. If humans knew we could read and write, they'd be plenty scared. They'd be afraid we'd try to take over the world. That's what my mom told me.

Since I like water so much, I'm happiest spending my time on the wharves here in Pittsburgh, with the other neighborhood dogs and my family.

Every day my buddies and I watch the big ships come in. We listen to the tales the sailors tell. We hear more stories from the folks who live near the wharves.

I like listening to adventure tales. But I don't ever want to have an adventure myself. There are a lot of scary things in the world. Why go looking for trouble?

July 10, 1803

The Pittsburgh wharves

Today I met a man named Meriwether Lewis. I was swimming along, minding my own business, while my friends and family played on the wharf. Suddenly, I noticed a really tall man watching me.

I don't know why, but I started showing off for him. I swam faster and faster. I dove deep under the water. Then I paddled over the waves. I fairly flew out of the water and jumped onto the wharf. When I was in front of the man, I gave myself a good shake.

The man just stood there and laughed. He even gave me a pat on the head. Then the man, who introduced himself as Meriwether Lewis, started talking to Emmett, the retired sailor who lives with my family and me. (Well, I guess since it is his house, *we* live with *him*.)

Lewis told Emmett that he was looking for a brave dog like me. Emmett looked at me, then back at Lewis. "Huh?" Emmett said. He knows I am the opposite of brave.

Lewis told him he wanted a dog who liked the water and could hunt and be a watchdog. Lewis said he was an explorer and was getting a crew together. He explained that he had come to the Pittsburgh wharves to have a special boat built. He called it a keelboat. He and his team were going to take it across the continent on rivers.

Emmett looked at Lewis like he was crazy, until Lewis started talking about money. Suddenly, Emmett started telling Lewis that I was a great hunter, a fierce watchdog, and a real hero. None of it was true. But he got Lewis to offer more and more money, until finally he offered a whopping 20 dollars for me. That's a lot of money for a dog!

I could tell Emmett liked what he heard. But he told Lewis he'd think about it overnight and would meet him at the docks the next morning. Now I'm at home, and I still can't believe what has happened. I hope Emmett decides not to sell me. It sounds like Lewis plans to take me on that trip with him. I overheard Emmett tell Lewis that he was crazy to try to cross the continent. "Who knows what is west of the Mississippi River?" Emmett said. He'd heard stories that there were woolly mammoths running around. He said there were unicorns, beavers that were seven feet tall, and volcanoes that erupted all the time! But Lewis just shook his head. (It wasn't so silly to think woolly mammoths lived in 1803. Most people didn't know at the time that animals became extinct. — Elvis)

I'm scared out of my wits. Tomorrow I might belong to a complete stranger, and then I'll have to journey with him into unknown and dangerous territory — for no good reason! But I guess I have no choice. If Emmett sells me, I have to go.

Tonight I told my parents how frightened I am. The last thing I want is to go on a trip. But my mother told me I should stay strong and keep writing in my diary. Dad said that sometimes humans get carried away making up scary stories and that I shouldn't worry about volcanoes or giant beavers. They both said that if I go, I'll learn a lot about myself, and that I'll find out I'm braver than I know. But I don't want to be brave. I want to stay in Pittsburgh.

July 11, 1803

Pittsburgh

Well, it happened. Emmett brought me back to the wharves this morning, and I now officially belong to Meriwether Lewis. I had to say good-bye to my friends and family. I don't know if I'll ever see them again.

I spent the day with Lewis. He is overseeing the construction of the keelboat. I'm a little less sad now because it turns out Lewis is a pretty nice guy. He talks to me like I'm his equal and explains things to me. The first thing he explained was the story behind his expedition. Now at least I know why he's going.

Lewis is friends with the president of the United States, Thomas Jefferson. Lewis even used to work for President Jefferson! The president just bought a bunch of land west of the Mississippi River. Lewis calls this land, which was purchased for the country to make it bigger, the Louisiana Purchase. Now President Jefferson wants to find out everything he can about the land out West — the plants, the animals, and all the Native American tribes who live there. Jefferson also wants the Native American tribes to make peace. He knows that many of them are fighting with one another. But if they were at peace, it would be safe for everyone to travel across the country. Plus, President Jefferson figures the country will just keep getting bigger. So he wants to find a water route from coast to coast so it will be easy for people to travel and transport goods. Lewis calls this water route the Northwest Passage.

After Lewis explained all this, I barked at him as if to ask, "Where do *you* come in?" It was almost like Lewis understood me because he went on to say that Jefferson chose *him* to lead a group of men, called the Corps of Discovery, to journey out West, explore the land, meet the Native Americans, and search for the Northwest Passage. Lewis then chose another friend, Captain William Clark, to help him head up the voyage.

Lewis and Clark became friends when they were in the army. Lewis knew he would need a lot of help crossing the unknown territory. He thought so highly of Captain Clark that he knew he could trust him with his life. Lewis wrote Clark a letter asking him to join the expedition. Captain Clark accepted because he thought highly of Lewis, too!

Lewis also explained that he had chosen me to help him on his journey. He said he's counting on me to protect the men from whatever strange animals and ferocious warriors we might find. Too bad that I'm no hero. The first time I come face-to-face with danger, I am going to turn my tail on it. As I said, I never wanted to go on a real adventure.

But I have to admit that a tiny part of me is proud that Lewis has picked me for this journey. Even if a bigger part of me is scared.

September 12, 1803

Camp Wood, on the Woods Hole River,
near St. Louis, Missouri, and the Missouri River

Two months have passed since I last wrote. I've been very busy, and so has Captain Lewis. We're slowly preparing for the big trip. Now we (and the rest of the Corps of Discovery) are camping at this place, Camp Wood, where we will train for the trip throughout the fall and winter. The river we are camping on runs into the Missouri River. That's where we will head once it's spring and the ice on the river has thawed. But I'm still not sure if I want to go. I've been thinking of escaping.

I'd feel bad if I snuck off, though. I really like Captain Lewis. He is one of the smartest men I have ever met. He is also honest and brave. Even though he is on the quiet side, I understand him, even if he's not saying much. This brings me to something new I've discovered: Human beings don't understand much about one another without words. They have to know one another's language in order to communicate. Dogs can understand each other, humans, and most other animals even if we don't all speak the same language.

Some of the men in the Corps of Discovery know more than one language. Some of them even know Native American languages. All that will come in handy where we are going. *If* I'm going. Which brings me back to my dilemma!

If I escape and go back to Pittsburgh, I think my parents will be disappointed in me. They told me to be brave. Also, the Corps of Discovery follows military law. This means that desertion is punishable by (*gulp*) death.

But if I stay, and go on the trip, then I'll really be putting my life in danger. It seems like I just can't win. Should I stay or go?

September 15, 1803

Camp Wood

Captain Lewis has been watching me pace back and forth. He knows something is wrong. But it is not what he thinks it is.

The captain keeps telling me to be patient. He says our adventure will begin soon. That's the last thing I want to hear.

Captain Clark, who is a little bit more talkative than Lewis, also wants to cheer me up. He keeps trying to get me to play fetch.

I think I've decided to go home. But I know I will miss Lewis and Clark.

September 20, 1803

Camp Wood

It's strange the way things turn out sometimes. Yesterday, I was determined to leave. Now I am determined to stay. I guess I have Moses Reed to thank.

Most of the guys in the Corps of Discovery are great. They are strong and brave and fun to be with, too. They're the kind of guys you can count on. (Go to the end of the book for a full list of the members of the Corps. — Elvis)

There is one member of the Corps I really dislike, though. His name is Moses Reed. He has a sly glint in his eyes. He reminds me of a wharf rat. I don't like the way he looks at me. He doesn't like me, either.

Last night I slipped away when nobody was looking. I sniffed my way along a trail that led away from camp. I kept thinking about Captain Lewis, Captain Clark, and the others. I wondered how long it would take before they realized I was gone.

I was about an hour out of camp when I saw him. Moses Reed. He looked at me with those rat eyes of his.

"What's the matter, you mangy mutt?" he said. "You chicken out on the captain?" Then he chuckled. It was a nasty sound.

"I can't blame you," he said. "I'm thinking about running off myself. I can make plenty of money trading fur up and down the river. Who needs to go running around the wilderness like a fool?"

I was surprised to find myself growling. Lewis and Clark and the others aren't fools. They are brave.

I may not want to be a hero, but I don't want to be like Moses Reed, either. So I turned around and trotted back to camp.

Captain Lewis, Captain Clark, and the others had been looking for me. They all were really glad to see me. I was glad to see them, too.

Reed tried to take credit for finding me. He told Captain Lewis that I was lost. The captain didn't believe him. He said I was just exploring.

I was glad that Captain Lewis stuck up for me. But it made me ashamed for thinking about running away, too. I'm definitely going on the trip now, no matter what.

CHAPTER 2
May 14–May 23, 1804

When spring came, the Corps of Discovery took off. Seaman was starting his adventure at last, even though he still had his worries.

May 14, 1804

Heading up the Missouri River

We're off! At four o'clock today we began our journey. We left our camp on the Woods Hole River. The keelboat turned onto the Missouri River and headed upstream about four miles. Behind us were two more boats we'd taken along. They are big, flat-bottomed canoes called pirogues.

I stood on the keelboat right between Captain Lewis and Captain Clark. As we shoved off, Captain Clark threw his head back and laughed. Captain Lewis did not make a sound. Still, I could tell how happy he was. It made me happy, too.

I hope we haven't forgotten anything. There is nowhere to go shopping in the wilderness. You have to take everything you'll need with you. Everything!

Pots and pans. Clothing and blankets. Cornmeal and flour. Scientific instruments, paper and pens, and loads of other stuff. We even have 193 pounds of portable soup (just add water and you've got a hot meal).

We also have presents for the Native American tribes we will meet. We have medals that show two hands clasping. The medals are supposed to show friendship.

You need a mighty big boat to carry this heavy cargo. That's what the keelboat is made for. It is 55 feet long and 8 feet wide. It can be rowed, sailed, towed, or pushed with poles.

The keelboat is built for more than moving cargo. It is built for protection. A swivel cannon is mounted on the bow. There are storage bins on both sides. The lids can be raised and used as shields. I hope we won't need to use them.

When we're on this and other rivers, we'll travel by boat. Sometimes we'll be on land, and then we'll walk and make camp. Lewis and Clark also want to buy horses.

May 19, 1804

Heading up the Missouri

I know the point of this trip is to find exciting new things. Frankly, I don't know how we'll find anything. We can't see through the swarms of gnats and mosquitoes. Clouds of them cover us all day. They get in our eyes, noses, ears, and mouths.

The men smear grease on their skin. Mosquitoes bite through it. They bite through my fur, too.

At night, bugs swarm all over the camp. We make smoky fires to drive them away. We sleep under mosquito netting.

The whole crew is covered with bites. All we can do is watch one another scratch.

The Missouri River is full of mud. It's dangerous, too. Besides the strong current rushing against us, the water is full of sandbars and floating logs. I guess if we don't get eaten alive by mosquitoes, we might just drown in the river.

Captain Lewis and Captain Clark try to cheer everybody up. They keep talking about how we're going to see sights no Americans have seen before.

Some adventure.

May 22, 1804

Heading up the Missouri

Today the current was so strong it nearly tipped over the boat. In fact, it nearly pitched *me* overboard! The men were busy pushing long poles against the riverbed, trying to keep the boat from sinking.

I felt myself sliding across the deck as the boat rocked from side to side. I kept slipping closer and closer to the edge. Just as I was about to be pitched overboard, I gave a mighty shove backward and braced myself. I stopped short and gazed down at the rushing water, breathing a sigh of relief.

One of the men was not so lucky. Suddenly, I saw him fly through the air and fall into the waves. It was Private Shannon, the youngest man in the expedition. It seemed nobody else saw him fall.

I barked, but the roar of rushing water was

louder than I was. Besides, everyone was busy trying to save the boat.

The next thing I knew, I was in the water. The strong current rushed against me, and the water pushed me under, farther and farther from the boat. Lucky for me I'm a great swimmer.

I looked around and saw Shannon bobbing in the rough water. He called to me. "Come on, Seaman! Come on!" he cried. Then the water closed over his head.

Somehow I became stronger than the current. It wasn't easy, but I swam against the river and got closer to Shannon.

I reached his side just as he went under for the third time. I grabbed his collar in my teeth and started swimming toward the boat.

A couple of the men on board spotted me and were there to pull Shannon out of the water. Then they pulled me on board, too.

I felt my paws on the solid deck once more. The strength ran out of me like water through a hole in a bucket. My legs turned to jelly and I collapsed.

Captain Lewis rushed to my side. He tied me fast to the boat with a stout piece of rope so I

couldn't slide off. Then he hurried back to help the men fight to keep the boat from capsizing.

Later, when the water was calmer, Captain Lewis untied me. "Well done!" he cried. "Well done!" echoed the other men.

"Well done!" whispered Private Shannon. Then he gave me a pat on the back. "There is no man in the Corps who is braver than you," he said.

It was only then that what had happened really sank in. I had saved someone from drowning. It was something that Mom and Dad told me Newfoundlands did all the time. It was one reason many ships carried them on board.

Private Shannon was smiling down at me, and I felt a warm glow. I'd done something scary, but I hadn't even felt frightened in the moment. Now I just felt happy.

May 23, 1804

Heading up the Missouri

I'm still worried that I won't make it back from this trip alive. We've barely started and twice I've almost been killed. The first time was when I saved Shannon. The second time was today.

Captain Lewis and I went exploring on the riverbank. We do that a lot while Captain Clark stays on the keelboat or one of the pirogues with the men. After we hunt or explore, we meet up with the boat again upstream.

Today we hiked higher and higher until we were way up on a cliff. Finally, we stopped to rest. The captain walked to the edge of the cliff and looked down. Then he called to me. "Seaman! Come and take a look at this view of the river. We must be a hundred feet above it."

I stayed right where I was. Standing at the edge of a cliff and looking down didn't appeal to me.

Then, right before my eyes, the ground beneath Captain Lewis's feet began to crumble. The cliff was sliding straight down into the Missouri River. Captain Lewis was sliding with it!

It all happened so fast, there was no time to think. I sprang toward the captain and tried to rescue him.

It was too late. In an instant, he had vanished.

The next thing I knew, the ground was sliding out from under me, too. I jumped back as fast as I could. I barely managed to scramble my way to solid ground. My heart was pounding so hard that I could barely breathe.

I was sure that Captain Lewis's body lay broken a hundred feet below me. I finally got the courage to creep carefully to the cliff's edge and look down.

What a miracle I saw! The captain was safe. Well, almost.

He had thrust his long knife into the side of the cliff. He was holding the knife handle tightly while his feet dangled in the air.

While I stared in disbelief, he pulled himself up, up, up the cliff, climbing hand over hand. When he was near enough, I reached over, grabbed his collar in my teeth, and pulled him up beside me.

Captain Lewis threw his arms around my shoulders. "Thank you, brave dog!" he said. "I saw you rush to save me!"

He was right. That was exactly what I had done. My head was reeling with disbelief.

I guess I *can* be brave after all. Maybe I'm starting to learn new things about myself, just as Captain Lewis is learning new things about the country.

CHAPTER 3

May 25–June 24, 1804

Seaman was learning more about himself every day. The Corps was now making its way up the Missouri River.

May 25, 1804

Heading up the Missouri

The night after I tried to save Captain Lewis, all the men told me I was a hero. York, the tall, dark-skinned man who does the cooking, gave me a big piece of meat.

"You are a real member of the Corps," he said. "Everybody looks out for everybody else."

I like York a lot, and not just for his cooking. We have fun together, too. He takes me on walks when he gathers wild plants for the crew to eat. While we walk he talks to me about all kinds of things. It's like he's talking to another person.

Today we went hunting for beaver. We swam to where a little creek branched off from the river. That is where we found a beaver dam.

York jumped out of the water and ran to where he had left his gun on the bank. "Go scare those beavers out of the water, Seaman," he said. "Beaver tail steaks are pretty good food, and everybody will be mighty hungry tonight."

I spent the next half hour swimming underwater, scaring beavers out of hiding. York hunted a bunch of them and cooked them for dinner. He was right. Beaver tail steak *is* good.

I have heard the men say York is Captain Clark's servant. It seems strange to me. Nobody treats him like a servant. He does the same work everybody else does. Like he said, we all have to look out for one another.

I keep a special lookout for Captain Lewis, though. After all, he is my best friend. I keep a special lookout for Private Shannon, too. He is the youngest, and now that I've rescued him, I want him to stay safe.

I am making friends, but I am still homesick. I miss my family and pals from Pittsburgh. I need animal friends. So far, I can't talk to any of the wild animals we've seen. Back home, I could talk easily to the cats that lived on the wharves. But maybe wild animals speak a language all their own.

Still, I'm actually having a good time on this trip. Who would have thought?

May 29, 1804

Heading up the Missouri

I have gotten the men into a regular morning routine. I bark to wake them at dawn. Then we get breakfast.

Moses Reed is always the last to get up. He pulls his bearskin blanket over his head. I have to bark and bark.

This morning he called me a mangy mutt again. Captain Lewis heard him. "Don't you dare talk to Seaman like that," he said quietly. I know that made Reed even madder. He kept his mouth shut, though. He knew better than to talk back to Captain Lewis.

Reed is sneaky as well as lazy. When he should be working, he whittles instead. It seems all he ever does is whittle. One thing is for sure. You can't whittle while you work.

I wonder how this bad apple got into the Corps? This morning at breakfast, I found out that Shannon and York are on to him.

"Just look at that lazy Reed. He sure can chow down," said Shannon.

"He'll cook his own goose soon enough." York nodded. "The captains will get wise to him."

When Reed came back for a second helping, York shook his head. "Nope. If you keep eating like that you're going to tire yourself out. You'll have to go back to bed, and then Seaman will have to wake you up all over again."

Reed didn't think it was funny, but York laughed and laughed. Shannon did, too. I just howled!

June 12, 1804

Heading up the Missouri

Today, while some of us were hiking, we ran into a man named Pierre Dorion. He is a fur trapper. He has a wild twinkle in his eye and a great loud voice.

At first Dorion figured me for something wild,

too. When he saw me, he pointed at me and stared. He asked the two captains, "What's that? Some kind of wild beast I haven't seen before?" Then he jumped behind a tree and pretended to be scared. "Don't let him come near me!" he cried.

Captain Clark burst out laughing. Then Captain Lewis did, too. Pretty soon everybody was laughing. I didn't see what was so funny. I'm not a wild beast. I'm a member of the Corps of Discovery.

I held my head up high. I stood tall. Then I gave Dorion a stern look.

Then Dorion started laughing, too. "I am only kidding, you big dog," he said. "I know that you are an explorer, too." He pointed to himself. "I am the one who looks like a wild beast."

I decided to be a good sport about the whole thing. After all, he was making fun of himself, too.

Pierre Dorion is French Canadian, but his mother was part of the Omaha tribe. His wife is Yankton Sioux.

Dorion warned us about another Sioux tribe, the Teton Sioux. He said they are not peaceful and are fierce fighters. Other tribes are afraid of them.

The captains shrugged off his warning. "The

noise from our cannon will scare off any trouble-makers," Captain Lewis told him.

Dorion just shook his head. "Don't be so sure," he said. "The Teton Sioux don't scare easily."

June 14, 1804

Heading up the Missouri

Pierre Dorion decided to be our guest for a while. I like having him on board. He calls me "big bear."

Dorion speaks English and French. He knows several Native American languages, plus sign language.

I understand all human languages. Most dogs can. I can also write in human language. And I can understand most animals. But when it comes to the language of *wild* animals, though, I'm stumped.

June 17, 1804

Heading up the Missouri

Mom always told me, "Eat your veggies." She was right. The men aren't getting enough fresh vegetables. It isn't good for their health. Neither is the muddy river water.

All of the men have boils and blisters. Captain Lewis says everyone is as sick as a dog. That doesn't make any sense. I'm a dog, and I'm not sick.

June 24, 1804

Heading up the Missouri

Last night I had a close call. Moses Reed caught me writing in my diary. I sat on it really fast, but it was too late. Reed ran off and came back with the captains.

"That dog was writing!" he said, pointing to me. "I saw him! Dogs are smarter than we thought. They'll try to take over the world! We've got to stop them!"

Everyone heard him yelling, and a crowd began to gather.

"Was the dog writing you a letter?" Private Shannon asked with a chuckle.

"Maybe you're still asleep and you're dreaming," said York.

"Ooh la la," said Pierre Dorion.

Captain Clark started laughing. But Lewis was angry.

"We don't have time for jokes," he said. "Go do some work!" Then he patted me on the head.

Reed tried to argue. The captains wouldn't listen, thank goodness. I'll have to be more careful from now on.

CHAPTER 4

June 30 – August 28, 1804

Before Seaman met his first Native American tribes, everyone was worried. Would they be friendly, or would they attack?

June 30, 1804

The Corps has reached Kansas.

It turns out Lewis and Clark are also keeping journals.

The other day I snuck a peek at Captain Lewis's. *Uh-oh!*

I saw *beautiful* spelled "butifull." I saw *valleys* spelled "vallies." *The United States* was even spelled "The Un*tied* States."

How can such a smart man be a bad speller? I wish I could give him a lesson.

Captain Clark doesn't need any lessons in making maps. He sure knows what he's doing. He can even estimate distance by sight. It's called dead reckoning.

July 4, 1804

Camped out in Kansas

Today we celebrated our country's independence. It was exciting. To celebrate the Fourth of July, the men shot the cannon.

Boom!

"That sound won't scare the Teton Sioux when we meet up with them," said Pierre Dorion.

I remembered that President Jefferson wanted the tribes to be peaceful. I hope that they turn out to be.

July 25, 1804

The Corps of Discovery has reached Nebraska.

We have reached the Platte River. It is a mile wide but only an inch deep!

We still haven't met any Native American tribes. We have seen new animals, though. Among them are the Plains horned toad and the Eastern wood rat. I made up the names myself, depending on how the creatures looked. I couldn't talk to any of them, though.

July 31, 1804

Nebraska

Yesterday I went hunting with Captain Lewis. When I saw something scurrying up ahead, I took off. I thought: *Maybe this one I can talk to!*

"Leave that little critter alone, Seaman," Lewis called to me. "We need bigger game."

But I just kept running.

"Hey, you! Come back here!" I barked at the critter. "I just want to talk to you."

He kept on going.

It took some doing, but I finally caught him. He had short legs and a white stripe on his head. "Tell me about yourself," I barked.

But he just made some noise. More gibberish.

Captain Lewis was angry that I ran away from him. But when he saw the little animal, he forgot all about it. Finding new animals is important. But was he new, or was he just an ordinary ground-hog? We weren't sure.

We took him back to camp. The French boatmen said it was a badger.

Nobody in the Corps had seen one before. That meant I had found a new animal!

"Good job, Sea," said Captain Lewis.

"Fine work," said Captain Clark.

I got lots of compliments from the other men. I'm glad they couldn't see me blushing under my fur. I guess it *was* pretty brave of me to go after the badger!

August 2, 1804

Nebraska, near the Iowa border

Today we met Native Americans! Two of them came to our camp. They were from the Otoe and Missouri tribes.

We gave them some pork and lard. They gave us some watermelons. (Oh, dear. Captain Clark spelled it "water millions" in his journal.)

I was having a fine time, until something awful happened. One of the men asked Captain Lewis when he would roast me.

I don't like being mistaken for livestock. Captain Lewis didn't like it, either. He set them

straight. He told him I was a soldier with the Corps.

It turns out that the Otoe and Missouri tribes eat dog. They say other tribes do, too.

I am still going to try to make Native American friends. But anybody who tries to make a meal out of me will be sorry!

August 3, 1804

Camped out in Nebraska

This morning about 250 people from the Otoe and Missouri tribes rode into our camp. They were having a meeting with the Corps.

They all wore buckskin pants and their shirts were decorated with porcupine quills. Some of them had painted designs on their bodies. The chiefs had headdresses of many feathers.

The captains wore their best clothes. Captain Lewis made a speech and Captain Clark gave out the gifts.

The speech told how this land was now part of the United States. The president wanted all the tribes to be peaceful. If they kept fighting with one another, they would be punished.

That made sense to me. A land full of fighting isn't safe for travel. Anyway, peace is a good thing.

"What a crazy idea," said a boy named Wind Runner. "How can men show bravery if they don't fight? How will they win honor? How will they become chiefs?"

That gave me something to think about. I had figured that *everybody* would want to be peaceful. But if Native American men got to be chiefs by fighting, how could peace work?

Wind Runner said he had something to show me. I went with him because I was curious and because he promised not to eat me.

He took me to a cave and showed me beautiful paintings his tribe had made on the walls. The pictures told stories of ceremonies and battles.

"See?" he said. "It is important to show bravery in battle. Smallpox killed many of my people. Now we fear other tribes. One day I will be chief and lead my people in battle once more."

Then he took me to his village. His people live in big lodges made of timber covered with earth. Twice a year they leave to hunt buffalo.

I met some Otoe and Missouri dogs. They

weren't like any dogs I knew. They were more like wild animals and didn't speak to me. I felt sorry for them — they may become dinner any day!

August 4, 1804

Heading up the Missouri

The Otoe and Missouri liked the gifts the Corps gave them. But they were really hoping for rifles, ammunition, and other things they could use. We didn't have enough space to carry those things. We had just enough for ourselves.

I learned a lot from Wind Runner. I wonder about the next tribe we will meet.

August 7, 1804

Heading up the Missouri

Moses Reed lied to Captain Lewis. He told him he had left his knife at our last camp, but I saw him whittling all evening.

Captain Lewis told him to go get his knife. He also told him to come back quickly. That was four days ago. He still has not returned.

"That fool thinks he's slick," York said. "But he's taking a big chance."

It's true. The law says deserters can be killed. That is because everybody has to be able to count on one another. Even though I don't like Reed, I wouldn't want him to be killed.

August 16, 1804

Iowa, near the Nebraska border

One of the men is very, very sick. His name is Private Charles Floyd.

I go to see him many times every day. All I can do is lick his face. York sits by his side.

Captain Lewis tries to tend to him. Nothing helps.

Every night Captain Clark stares up at the sky. I know he is very worried. So am I.

August 17, 1804

Camped out in Nebraska

This evening George Drouillard brought Reed back to camp. He confessed to deserting and to stealing a rifle.

Reed has been thrown out of the Corps. He will be sent back to St. Louis in the spring. I think that's good. He doesn't belong in the Corps. Meanwhile, I hope he stays away from me.

August 20, 1804

Heading up the Missouri

This was a very sad day. Private Charles Floyd died. He had appendicitis. There was nothing we could have done to save him.

We buried him high up on a hill. There was a beautiful view of the Missouri River. I like to think that he can see it.

Captain Clark put a cedar post over his grave. They named a branch of the river Floyd's River, and they also called the hill Floyd's Bluff.

Everyone was very quiet for a long, long time.

August 23, 1804

Heading up the Missouri

Out here we never know what will happen next. Sometimes it is bad. Sometimes it is good. Today it was good.

Sergeant Joseph Field went hunting. A few hours later I heard him yelling from the riverbank.

I barked back and ran to meet him. He was

jumping up and down and waving his arms around.

"I got a buffalo! I got a buffalo!" he said. "We're having buffalo for dinner!"

I'd never tasted buffalo. None of the Corps had. We had heard about it, though. Dorion said it was better than beaver tail.

Ha! I didn't believe that one. I thought nothing could be better than beaver tail steak. I was wrong, though. Buffalo *is* better than beaver tail steak.

We had a real feast tonight. Everyone ate buffalo hump, buffalo tongue, and buffalo steak.

For a while the food cheered us up a little. But after the meal everyone went off alone. We were all thinking about Private Floyd.

August 27, 1804

South Dakota

We have entered a new kind of country. It is called the Great Plains. It is also Sioux country.

There is something spooky about it. There is nothing but grass as far as the eye can see. No trees except for a few cottonwoods lining the riverbank.

Last night Private Shannon rode away from

camp. He did not come back. He must be lost. What if some angry warriors find him?

Tomorrow we are meeting the Yankton Sioux. That is the tribe of Pierre Dorion's wife.

August 28, 1804

Heading up the Missouri

Today, the Yankton Sioux arrived with four musicians in the lead. They were singing and playing. Next came the chiefs and warriors.

Everyone wore buffalo robes of different colors and feathers. The chiefs wore the most feathers of all.

The day started with the Corps' full-dress parade, Captain Lewis's speech about peace, and the captains giving out presents.

Then the meeting turned into a big party. Boys did trick shots with bows and arrows. And they all wanted to pet the "big dog that looks like a bear." I let them.

At sundown, the Yankton prepared a feast. Too bad dog was on the menu.

It gave me the creeps.

I went outside and sat by myself. After a while

a Yankton girl came over. She had brought me some food.

"Go ahead, eat," she told me. "It's buffalo. I don't like dog, either."

The girl's name was Morning Star. When I finished eating, she led me to the center of camp. Three big fires burned there.

The Yankton put on the best show I have ever seen. Painted men leaped in the firelight. They danced and sang about bravery in battle. Others made music with deer-hoof rattles and drums.

It was a magical day. And I realized I'd hardly been scared once.

CHAPTER 5
August 29–
September 20, 1804

After waiting for a long time, Seaman finally found a new animal to talk to.

September 5, 1804

Heading up the Missouri

We have been searching for Private Shannon. There is no sign of him. We are all worried about him.

September 6, 1804

Heading up the Missouri

I got some men to come looking with me today. We still didn't find Shannon. One of the men was Pierre Dorion. He was nearly the next member of the Corps of Discovery to die. Here is how it happened:

Dorion and I split off from the others. The two of us were busy looking for tracks. We didn't hear rustling in the grass until it was almost too late.

Usually, Dorion would have spotted the snake right away. He is a great outdoorsman. But I guess he was worried about Shannon, so he was distracted.

All of a sudden, we came face-to-face with a huge snake. His little red eyes looked like they were on fire. He made an awful noise, a hissing sound. I had never heard it or seen a snake's forked tongue before, but I knew it meant trouble.

Then something very unusual happened. Pierre Dorion was so shocked he dropped his rifle. That surprised me because I had never seen him get rattled. Each time he tried to pick up the gun, the snake's head shot toward him.

Neither one of us made a sound.

Dorion took a step backward. The snake's hissing got louder. I saw his whole body stiffen, and I knew he was ready to strike.

I heard my own roar before I knew I was barking.

Now the snake was looking at me. I kept barking at the snake, to hold its attention on me. When I heard Dorion pick up his rifle, I turned and ran.

Boom! I heard the shotgun blast, then Dorion's voice calling my name.

I kept on running, but not for long. I realized that Dorion had shot the snake. It just took a moment to sink in.

Whew! The meeting with the snake taught me a lesson. Out here you have to be alert all the time. If you're not paying attention, even for a second, that second might be your last.

September 7, 1904

Heading up the Missouri

Pierre Dorion has decided to stay with the Yankton. I will miss him.

Today Lewis and I went walking with some of the men. As usual, Captain Clark stayed on board while the men rowed and pushed the boat upstream.

Lewis and I were on the lookout for more new animals. And we found them — a whole little village of them that lived underground!

First one popped out, then another and another. There were thousands of them.

I ran toward one. *Poof!* It was gone. It happened again.

And again.

And again.

I felt pretty foolish, running this way and that. The men were doing the same thing. The little rascals were driving us nuts.

Jump up. Chatter, chatter, chatter. Jump down into the tunnel.

Suddenly, I realized that I understood what they were saying! Once more, I tried to catch one.

Nyah, nyah, nyahnyahnyah. You can't catch me.

This time I tried harder.

Ha-ha-ha! Fooled ya! he chattered before he disappeared.

The men tried digging into their tunnels. But they were much too deep.

Then I had an idea. I ran back to the boat. I found a bucket and filled it with water. I carried it in my mouth to Captain Lewis.

"Good thinking!" he told me. "A dunking will force one out."

But it took a lot more than a bucket's worth of dunking. It took five barrels. Finally, a soggy little chatterbox crawled out.

Ha-ha-ha! I barked at him. *Who has the last laugh?*

Nobody teases Seaman and gets away with it.

September 8, 1804

Heading up the Missouri

This morning I went to see the little guy we caught. He was in a cage. He looked so sad that I felt sorry for him.

"What kind of animal are you?" I asked.

"A dog," he said.

"You can't be a dog," I told him. "I'm a dog."

He got all snooty. "I'm a *prairie dog,* mister smarty-paws," he said. "French trappers call me *petit chien.* That's French for 'little dog.'"

Just my luck. At last I've met a wild animal I can talk to, and he's a smart aleck. I'm a dog, and he doesn't look like me.

Later on I got to thinking. He was the only wild animal I understood. Maybe he *was* some kind of dog after all. (No matter what the prairie dog said, a prairie dog is not a dog. It is a member of the squirrel family. Prairie dog language is about as complex as dolphin language. — Elvis)

I guess I'll try harder to make friends with him. I sure have been waiting for an animal friend.

September 9, 1804

Heading up the Missouri

We are in a beautiful part of the country. There is nothing like it back in Pittsburgh.

We have seen huge herds of buffalo, deer, and elk. Birds as big as men make strange whooping sounds. I call them whooping cranes. Hawks circle overhead, always on the lookout for prey.

There is plenty of game for us all. It's a good thing, too. The men work so hard. They each need about nine pounds of meat a day to keep their up strength!

Every night, I sit out and stare at the stars. I wonder what everybody is doing back in Pittsburgh. I wonder if they think about me.

The only sore spot in all this is that Shannon is still missing. And now the prairie dog refuses to speak to me.

September 10, 1804

Heading up the Missouri

Today I went exploring with Captain Clark. I found a backbone that was 45 feet long. There were pieces of jawbone and teeth, too.

Captain Clark and I just stared. It was a fossil of some animal that lived long ago. From the looks of it, it was a gigantic fish.

Captain Clark said it meant the land where we were standing was once covered with water. Lots of it. Enough for a 45-foot fish to swim in.

"Bet you couldn't eat a fish that big," Clark said to me.

He's right.

September 13, 1804

Heading up the Missouri

We found Shannon a couple of days ago! Our boat rounded a bend in the river. Suddenly, there he was, sitting right there on the riverbank.

I jumped into the water and swam right to him. He gave me a big hug and petted me.

"It sure is great to see you," he said. His voice

was almost a whisper. He was thin and very weak. It turned out he'd gotten lost. After he got lost, he lost his ammunition, too. He couldn't hunt. That meant he couldn't eat.

He managed to catch a rabbit, and he found some grapes. That was all he had eaten in 12 days. He was lucky he wasn't eaten himself by wild animals!

September 15, 1804

Heading up the Missouri

We have been speeding along, getting closer and closer to where the Mandan tribe make their home.

We have seen so many new animals. The prairie dog is still the only one I can understand, but he still refuses to talk to me.

One of the new animals looked like a deer but had ears like a mule. I tried to make friends, but she ran away.

Another looked like a rabbit, only bigger. I never saw a rabbit jump so far. It leaped at least 20 feet.

Today I saw another creature that looked like a cross between a goat and an antelope. I chased after it. It left me in the dust. I'll bet that animal was going 70 miles per hour. It had horns, a black mask on its face, and a tan coat. There were two white bands across its throat. After it took off, all I saw was its white tail.

September 16, 1804

Heading up the Missouri

I finally got a few words out of the prairie dog. He isn't snooty after all. He's just homesick. I should have known.

I tried to cheer him up. I told him that I was far from home, too. I told him about being an explorer. "You'll like seeing new sights," I said.

He wasn't so sure, but it broke the ice. Soon we were chatting away.

"Why are all these wild animals so unfriendly?" I asked. I told him about the animals I had seen. I had made up names for them all.

Mule deer.

Jackrabbit.

Pronghorn antelope.

(The names that Seaman gave to these new animals actually became their real, recorded names! — Elvis)

"Why won't they talk to me?" I asked.

The little dog just wrinkled his nose. "They are *wild* animals. They aren't civilized, like us dogs. Besides, word gets around on the prairie. They know you've had some of them for dinner."

I guess I hadn't thought of that. Of course they wouldn't like me. They thought I was hunting. But I wasn't hunting all *those* animals. I only hunt animals the men and I need for dinner.

Anyway, at least I learned the prairie dog's name. It's Marcel.

September 20, 1804

Heading up the Missouri

Now Marcel and I get along really well.

When Lewis saw how friendly we were, he let Marcel out of his cage. "Keep an eye on him," he told me. "Don't let him run away."

Marcel promised he wouldn't. He likes being an explorer if he doesn't have to stay in a cage.

CHAPTER 6
September 22– October 23, 1804

When the Corps of Discovery finally met up with the Teton Sioux, it's a good thing Seaman had gotten used to danger. He got a double dose of it.

September 22, 1804

Heading up the Missouri

I told Marcel we would meet up with the Teton Sioux pretty soon. He stood on his hind legs and thrust his front paws out. He started to chatter. That is what nervous prairie dogs do.

"Forget it!" he said. "I want them to stay away!"

I explained that wouldn't be possible. The president wanted us to get everybody to make friends.

"Phooey!" said Marcel. "You're in for big trouble!"

September 25, 1804

Heading up the Missouri

Today we met the Teton Sioux and held a council with them.

After Captain Lewis gave his usual speech, Captain Clark handed out gifts.

Marcel got up on his hind legs and started to chatter. "*Uh-oh.* We're in for it now!"

Sure enough, things started to go bad.

The three chiefs — Black Buffalo, Black Medicine, and the Partisan — all got medals. Black Buffalo got a military coat and a three-cornered hat, too. That made Black Medicine angry. The Partisan was *furious.* All three chiefs complained about the gifts. "This is it? A bunch of medals and a silly hat?" they grumbled.

The captains tried to save the day. They invited the chiefs to visit the keelboat.

But when it came time to go, the Partisan wouldn't leave.

By now I was mad enough to bite them all. I

didn't dare. About 50 or 60 Teton warriors were watching our every move.

Finally, the captains coaxed the chiefs into a pirogue. Captain Clark and a couple of men rowed them to shore.

But then three warriors grabbed the pirogue and wouldn't let go.

This time, the Teton Sioux had pushed Captain Clark too far. He drew his sword and ordered his men to shoulder their rifles.

On the keelboat, Lewis ordered the men to take up arms. He stood ready to fire the cannon.

The warriors on shore raised their bows. Any moment, arrows and bullets would fly. I was in the middle of my worst nightmare.

The Teton Sioux were acting like bullies. I don't like bullies, so I decided to do something about it. I was scared but also angry.

I jumped into the water, I swam to Black Buffalo, and I looked him right in the eye. I barked angrily at him, as if to say, "Be nice to us. We are trying to be your friends."

Black Buffalo looked back at me. He didn't say anything, but I could tell he was rethinking his actions. Then he walked to the pirogue. He ordered the braves to let go. They obeyed.

But the trouble did not end there. As we rowed away from shore, Black Buffalo and some warriors waded after us. They begged to come back to the keelboat. They wanted to ride in it.

Captain Clark still wanted us all to be friends, so he took them back to the boat.

September 27, 1804

Camping near the Teton Sioux

Two weeks ago, before we even met them, the Teton won a battle with the Omaha. They captured 25 women and made them slaves. Now they are having parties to celebrate. We went to one of them.

The captains and the chiefs sat in a circle and smoked a pipe. The captains tried to talk about peace. They said the Teton should release the slaves.

Then the Teton women started to dance. The men sang songs. They were all about battle.

While this was going on, Omaha slave women served the Teton. When one of the women struggled with a heavy pot, York went to help her. The Teton stared in surprise. They had never seen anyone with black skin like York. They thought he might be magical, and asked why such a big magic man would help a slave woman.

The captains tossed presents to the singers and dancers. One dancer didn't think he got enough. He got angry. He broke a drum and flung it into the fire. Then he stormed away.

I held my breath, but nothing else happened. Everybody just went on with the party. *Whew.*

September 29, 1804
Heading up the Missouri

We have finally said good-bye to the Teton Sioux. I'm so relieved. I have been worried for days.

Fall is beginning. The Plains are turning golden. Overhead, flocks of ducks and geese are flying south. The sound of honking and quacking fills the air.

"What waits for us up the Missouri?" I asked Marcel. He told me the answer.

Soon we will be meeting the Arikara tribe.

He heard about them through the prairie dog grapevine.

The Arikara are farmers. They pretty much live in one place. Most of their tribe was killed by the smallpox epidemic. That reminds me of the Otoe and Missouri tribes.

"The Arikara are nice folks," Marcel told me. "All we prairie dogs like them, and they like us."

I hope they'll like the rest of us, too. After what happened with the Teton Sioux, we are all a little nervous.

October 8, 1804

Heading up the Missouri, near the North Dakota border

Today Captain Lewis pointed to an island. "That is where the Arikara live," he told me. "Come with me to meet them."

The two of us got into a pirogue. We took two boatmen who spoke Arikara with us. As we paddled over, I wondered what would happen.

I had nothing to worry about. The Arikara gave us a warm welcome. A 13-year-old girl with beautiful dark hair and shining eyes walked right up to me and patted my head. She told me her name was Moon Song. While Lewis arranged a meeting with the chiefs, she showed me around the island.

The place looks like a garden. When it comes to growing things, the Arikara know what they're doing. They raise corn and beans and squash and pumpkins. Moon Song told me they hunt buffalo, too.

October 10, 1804

Heading up the Missouri

We have said good-bye to the Arikara people and are on our way again. One of the chiefs is coming with us. He will talk with the Mandan about peace between the tribes.

Before we left, Moon Song warned me about something. "Don't hunt the grizzly bear," she said. "They are very bad medicine."

Other members of the tribe also warned the captains. I think they know what they're talking about. They have seen grizzlies.

Marcel has seen the grizzlies, too. He says the men will be sorry if they take on one of them. I hope it never happens.

October 20, 1804

The Corps of Discovery reaches North Dakota.

It happened. Pierre Cruzatte and I were hunting today. We saw giant bear tracks. We knew they belonged to a grizzly bear.

I wanted to get as far away from the bear as possible. What did Cruzatte want to do? He wanted to find it. So we followed the tracks. But when we came upon the bear, he was none too happy to see us. He roared.

It was too late to run. Cruzatte raised his rifle and fired.

He is a great fiddle player, but not much of a shot. He wounded the bear, which made the bear even madder. He kept on coming at us, roaring.

And roaring.

We turned and started to run. The bear kept roaring along behind us. He sounded as loud as our cannon.

It's a miracle that we got away. Running from a

bear isn't a good idea, because bears are very fast. This means you usually get caught.

Pierre Cruzatte ran up a tree. I squeezed into a hole. That bear stayed around and roared and pawed at us for a couple of hours. I thanked my lucky stars when he finally got tired, gave up, and went away.

I hope Cruzatte learned his lesson. I learned that I *don't* want to mess with any more grizzly bears.

October 23, 1804

Heading up the Missouri

This morning it snowed. Marcel and I played tag in it. Shannon and York watched us, laughing.

The temperature is dropping fast. Captain Lewis says that there will be ice on the river soon. We will not be able to travel on it until the spring thaw.

We're going to spend the winter with the Mandan tribe. Their friends, the Hidatsa, live nearby.

I realized that I have actually been enjoying traveling. Now it is getting cold, though, and I am ready for a rest.

CHAPTER 7

October 24, 1804 – April 8, 1805

When Seaman met a kind Native American girl, he couldn't guess how much she'd help the expedition.

October 24, 1804

North Dakota near the Mandan tribe's camp

Today we met members of the Mandan tribe. They wore buckskin clothing decorated with porcupine quills and paint. Their faces were painted with red dye. Some of the men even painted their hair red. Chiefs wore big headdresses with horns, and warriors had eagle feathers in their long hair.

The women wore their hair parted and braided. They painted the part with red dye. The Mandan chief, Big White, talked about peace with the Arikara chief. He said they would try to get their tribes to be friendly. I hope it works.

October 30, 1804

Camping with the Mandan

Mandan houses are made for long, hard winters. They are dome-shaped lodges of wood and earth. They hold in the heat from a big fire in the center. Smoke passes through a hole at the top. There is room inside for several families and their horses, too.

It's starting to get very cold. Even my fur doesn't keep me warm. Soon the Corps will begin building a fort. I think we should try to make it like the Mandan lodges. Marcel disagrees. He wants to have an underground burrow.

November 3, 1804

Camping with the Mandan

We have begun building our fort. It won't look like the Mandan lodges. It won't be a burrow, either. It will be made of logs.

The captains spend lots of time visiting with the Mandan and Hidatsa chiefs. They ask about the places we'll go and the tribes we'll meet.

Marcel and I always listen in. We've learned that there is a big, big waterfall on the Missouri. The source of the river is in the Rocky Mountains. We'll have to cross them to get to the Columbia River. To do that, we'll need horses.

Where will we get the horses?

From the Shoshone. They live at the foot of the Rockies. They are poor, but they have good horses. That is what the chiefs said.

"It might not be so easy to get horses from the Shoshone," I heard Captain Lewis say to Clark. "They might not want to trade with us. None of us know how to speak Shoshone, either."

I know that without horses there is no way we'll get over the mountains. Then the expedition will fail.

November 4, 1804

Camping with the Mandan

Today I met a girl named Sacagawea. Her name means "bird woman," and she is going to have a baby in a few months.

Sacagawea is only 14 years old. I see many more years of wisdom in her kind eyes.

Her husband is a French Canadian trapper named Toussaint Charbonneau. He has lived with the Hidatsa for years. He speaks their language and French. I think he's a lot older than Sacagawea is.

Charbonneau came to see Lewis and Clark last week. He wants to join the expedition and be an interpreter. He told us that he could do all kinds of things. He said he was an experienced boatman, a terrific trapper, and a great cook.

The more he talked, the more he puffed out his chest. The way he did that made me think he might be fibbing.

Then Charbonneau said his young wife was from the Shoshone tribe. The captains told him to bring her along on the trip.

November 14, 1804

Camping with the Mandan

Things have a way of working out. Sacagawea speaks Hidatsa *and* Shoshone. She can help us make friends with her people and trade for the horses we need.

The captains have another reason for wanting Sacagawea along. War parties do not travel with women and babies. Sacagawea and her infant, when it is born, will show the tribes that we are friendly.

December 3, 1804

Camping with the Mandan

We have moved into our winter quarters. There are two rows of lodges. Each one is about 14 feet square.

"Phooey!" Marcel says all the time. The split-log floor is cold, but when he's near the fire he's too hot.

What bothers me is feeling cooped up in the small room. It's smoky, too. At night the light from the candles is dim. It's hard to write in secret, and now it's hard to see, too.

December 6, 1804

Camping with the Mandan

Captain Lewis has been keeping a diary of the weather. Lately it has been about four degrees above zero. Icy winds blow almost all the time. The river is frozen solid.

Marcel and I have our fur coats to keep us

warm, but we still feel cold. The men wear buckskin clothing and fur-lined moccasins. They wrap themselves in buffalo robes.

December 16, 1804

Camping with the Mandan

Today Marcel and I followed the Mandan and some of our men on a buffalo hunt. The Mandan are amazing horse riders. They guide the horses with their knees and ride at breakneck speed. They don't use reins. Their hands are free to shoot their arrows.

The captains and other men were amazed. "Look, Ma, no hands. How about that?" Captain Clark laughed.

The Mandan camped out all night. The captains and the other men stayed with them. Marcel and I came home. It was just too cold. That night the temperature dropped to 45 degrees below zero.

December 25, 1804

Camping with the Mandan

It's Christmas! This morning the men fired the cannon three times. Afterward, they raised the flag over the fort.

Marcel and I went to visit Sacagawea. She likes to play fetch with us. The way Marcel rolls in the snow makes her laugh. She calls me "Bear-Dog."

Today she gave us some sugar. She'd never tasted it until traders brought it to the Hidatsa village. Now it's her favorite treat. Marcel and I decided it was ours now, too.

January 25, 1805

Camping with the Mandan

A lot of time has passed since I last had a chance to write. We are still with the Mandan, and it's been great. Marcel and I play with the kids. Two have become our special friends. They are Snow Cat and his sister, Raven Wing.

Sometimes we visit their lodge. Raven Wing showed me her dollhouse made of willow branches. She says she can paddle a boat almost as well as her mother.

Snow Cat practices his riding almost every day. He wants to be a great hunter.

Snow Cat and Raven Wing call the captains by their Mandan nicknames. Captain Lewis is "Long Knife" and Captain Clark is "Red Hair."

February 5, 1805

Camping with the Mandan

The hunting isn't too good now. We have to go farther and farther into the woods to get enough meat for the men.

Private Shields, our blacksmith, found a way to help us get food. He mends hoes and sharpens axes for the Mandan. In return, they give us corn and beans.

Sacagawea sings as she does her chores. She says her baby is due soon.

Captain Clark won't let her lift anything heavy. He helps her a lot. During the past few months they have become good friends. He calls her Janey, because Sacagawea is hard for him to say.

February 11, 1805

Camping with the Mandan

Today Sacagawea's son was born! His name is Jean Baptiste Charbonneau. Captain Lewis delivered the baby.

The captain did such a good job, anyone would think he was a doctor. Sacagawea was very brave, too. I sat with her the whole time. She said I kept her calm and happy.

February 25, 1805

Camping with the Mandan

The baby's eyes sparkle like Sacagawea's. She smiles as she sings to him.

All the men love little Jean Baptiste, especially Captain Clark. He has nicknamed him Pomp.

I'd never seen a human baby before. "I can't believe he's so little," I told Marcel.

I am going to watch over him. He's now the youngest member of the Corps of Discovery. Someday he will know he was an important part of history.

March 11, 1805

Camping with the Mandan

When I got back from hunting today, Marcel was waiting outside the door. When I saw him up on his hind legs, I knew something was wrong. "The captains and Charbonneau are fighting," he said.

We went into the lodge to see what was going

on. Charbonneau was strutting around. He was demanding special treatment on the trip. He wanted: no working alongside the men, no hunting, and no guard duty. Plus, he wanted to be able to leave whenever he wanted.

The captains said no to everything. Then the argument started all over again. Round and round they went.

Then the captains said no for the last time. They dismissed Charbonneau from the expedition. They told him to leave Fort Mandan.

March 12, 1805

Camping with the Mandan

I saw Sacagawea walking with Pomp strapped to her back. Her face was like a stone. When I ran up to her, she smiled a little.

"I do not want to leave the expedition. I want to see my people again, Bear-Dog," she said. "I will not give up so easily."

Charbonneau passed by us. Sacagawea did not say a word. She would not look at him. When he walked away, his shoulders were sagging. I could not resist a growl.

"Don't be angry, Bear-Dog," she said. "My husband wants to feel important. Sometimes it makes him say silly things and make up stories." Then she followed him out of the camp. They've left. But I keep hoping that they will return.

March 14, 1805

Camping with the Mandan

I miss Pomp's giggles. I even miss his cries. I especially miss Sacagawea's light, sure steps. Both of the captains are worried, too. Will the Shoshone give us horses without Sacagawea? I hear them talking about it.

Meanwhile, the ice on the river is cracking. The boats need to be taken out of the river for repair.

The men try to hack the boats free with axes. They pour buckets of boiling water around the boats.

Once we set off, we will be seriously searching for the Northwest Passage.

March 17, 1805

Camping with the Mandan

Great news! Charbonneau has rejoined the expedition. Today he returned to camp with Sacagawea and Pomp. He agreed to follow the captains' rules. No special treatment.

My guess is that Sacagawea made him do it. She may be small, but she is tough. She is determined to travel with us to the Shoshone. When she makes up her mind to do something, it gets done. Sometimes I think her name should mean "iron woman" instead of "bird woman."

Everyone is happy to have them with us again. Now we will be able to get our horses from the Shoshone.

March 25, 1805

Camping with the Mandan

It took three weeks of hard work to pull the boats out of the ice. Now the men are repairing them. They are cutting trees to make canoes. Six new boats will be made.

Everyone works hard all day. They laugh and joke and sing. The air crackles with energy.

Marcel and I can't wait to get going. We talk about what we might see and do.

March 27, 1805

Camping with the Mandan

Today Marcel and I watched the men building canoes. We were so excited about the next part of our journey.

Then suddenly, everything changed. The captains came over and started talking about Marcel. They said he might have to travel in a cage again.

That is how we found out the bad news. Marcel and I will split up soon. He will be sent back to St. Louis on the keelboat. Then he will be sent on to Washington, D.C., to meet President Jefferson.

I'm sure that we will never see each other again.

April 5, 1805

Camping with the Mandan

Marcel and I spend hours talking. He wonders

about life in Washington. He wonders about the president. I tell him not to be afraid.

He says he will miss the wilderness. Even so, he is eager to see new sights. He says that I've made an explorer out of him. *Me!* And to think I was once afraid to be an explorer myself.

April 6, 1805

Camping with the Mandan

The keelboat will leave tomorrow. On board are the captains' notes, their drawings, and specimens of plants, animals, and insects. Bows and arrows and painted buffalo robes are there, too.

The canoes and pirogues will shove off tomorrow, too. It is our last night with the Mandan.

April 7, 1805

Camping with the Mandan

The keelboat has left with Marcel. A few other live animals we found and kept went with him. He'll travel with four magpies, another prairie dog, and a prairie hen.

I was very sad, and I told Marcel that I'd never

forget him. Then I gave him a letter. It was for my family back in Pittsburgh.

Marcel said he'd get the letter delivered somehow. He said that we'd always be friends. Then he promised to write.

When Marcel was getting on the boat, he turned back and chattered one last thing. He said he knew we'd see each other again.

April 8, 1805

Heading up the Missouri toward Montana

Our canoes shoved off yesterday after the keelboat left. I said good-bye to Snow Cat and the other Mandan. We are heading into the unknown.

Before, we had maps to follow. A few traders and trappers had traveled where we were traveling.

Now, we are heading into totally unmapped territory. We are making history.

CHAPTER 8
April 9–July 9, 1805

The Corps of Discovery left the Mandan camp and started on its journey once more. Seaman missed Marcel, but he had many other things to think about. Now they were really heading into the unknown.

April 9, 1805

Heading up the Missouri

Game is scarce. I am tired of parched corn and beef jerky.

When we stopped for dinner, Sacagawea called to me. "Come on, Bear-Dog. We're going hunting." *For what?* I wondered.

Sacagawea carried Pomp strapped to her back. As we walked, her eyes searched the ground.

After a while she stooped to pick up a sharp

stick. Then she began poking in the soft earth. "I'm looking for a nest of harvester mice," she said. "They store lots of delicious wild artichokes."

She found a nest and opened it. Little mice scurried out. The nest was filled with round white roots. She scooped them into a pouch, but left some for the mice.

I thought the mice looked mighty tasty. The next time she opened a nest, I pounced. I was fast, but the mice were faster. Sacagawea laughed as I lunged this way and that and never caught a single mouse.

It was five more nests before I caught a mouse. That's too much work for so little food. It's easier to catch squirrels or beavers. I'll bet it's even easier to catch a buffalo.

April 13, 1805

Yikes. Captain Lewis *almost* caught me writing in my diary last night. Now I'll have to be more careful than ever!

April 20, 1804

Heading up the Missouri

We have not met any new Native American tribes. Captain Lewis says he doesn't mind. We need to keep moving. We've got to get over the Rocky Mountains before winter. The captains are determined to find the Northwest Passage. It is a water route that explorers have dreamed of finding since the time of Christopher Columbus.

Lewis is always on the lookout for new animals. I'm good at finding them. Just the other day I spotted a goose sitting on a nest in the top of a cottonwood tree. I barked to alert the captain.

Back east, geese build their nests on the ground. It was smart for these wilderness geese to build them in trees. That way other animals couldn't get at them.

Captain Lewis thanked me for showing him the nest. He says I've discovered as many animals as anyone in the Corps.

Sometimes these animals surprise me. One of them was a little goose, not much bigger than a duck. He had a dark body and white stripes on his cheeks.

I thought a goose would be good for dinner. Before I could make a move, the little guy flew right at me. He made the most awful noise I've ever heard. That's why I call him a cackling goose.

I found another kind of goose, too. I like this one better. It's all white like the snow, except for black-tipped wings. It honks the way a goose should. I call it the snow goose.

May 19, 1805

North Dakota, Just over the Montana border

Something scary happened today when we went hunting beaver. After the hunters finished shooting, I jumped in the water to retrieve the animals. I've done it dozens of times before.

This time it was different. I chased a beaver that was wounded, not dead. When I lunged to grab it in my mouth, the beaver turned around. As it swam past me, I felt its razor-sharp teeth graze my leg.

The moment I felt the pain, I knew I'd better get to shore.

My leg was bleeding badly. It's a good thing I made it out of the water when I did. I am weak from losing so much blood. Captain Lewis bandaged my leg, but it is still very sore. I can see that he is worried.

Sacagawea sang to me and York brought me extra meat. I don't think I can write any more. I am very tired. . . .

May 27, 1805

Heading up the Missouri

I have been sick for days. All I could do was lie in the canoe. Most of the time I was dreaming. Sometimes I heard the captains talking, but they sounded far away. But I heard them say they were afraid I would die.

One day, I dreamed that I was walking into a fog. It got darker and darker all around me. I began to think I would never find my way out.

Just as I was about to give up, I saw a silver dog. She told me to follow her and that I would be all right. Then she led me out of the fog into a forest. Finally, we came to a beautiful meadow.

We lay down on the grass to rest. The dog began to disappear before my eyes. I fell asleep. When I woke up today, I was better. I stood up, and my leg hardly hurt at all.

When Captain Lewis saw me walking, his mouth dropped open. "I don't believe it," he gasped. "Whatever pulled you through, it was a miracle." I guess it was.

Sacagawea thought it was a special kind of miracle. She thought I was visited by a *wayakin* — a spirit guide. I listened while she told Captain Lewis about them.

In many tribes, when a boy or girl is about 13, they go off by themselves to fast and pray. They have a vision of a bird or animal. It is the spirit that will always watch over them — their *wayakin*.

I think Sacagawea is right. My *wayakin* came to visit me and saved my life.

May 29, 1805

Heading up the Missouri

It is a good thing that I am better. I have to protect everyone. Last night I saved the Corps from a wild beast!

I woke up and smelled a buffalo. Then I heard

him swimming in the river. I could tell that he was alone.

Why is he away from his herd? I wondered. *Is he crazy, or lost — or both?*

Then I heard the buffalo climb out of the water. He came charging right for the camp.

Sacagawea, Pomp, and the others were still sound asleep in their tents. Others slept on the ground outside. The buffalo's hooves pounded along near their heads.

I raced toward him, barking. I said something like, "Hey, get lost, you big hunk of meat, before you hurt somebody!"

Of course, he didn't understand me. He understood my nipping at his heels, though. I steered him right out of camp.

By then everybody was awake. They rubbed their eyes and watched me chase the buffalo. Their mouths were hanging open. I guess they were surprised that I wasn't scared of the big guy.

The buffalo had trampled a couple of rifles. He could have trampled some people. Everybody kept telling me how brave I was.

I have to say it feels nice. I'm not the same scared dog I was when I began this trip.

May 30, 1805

Heading up the Missouri

Yesterday, we passed by a river with clear water. Captain Clark named it "Judith's River" after his fiancée. They are going to be married as soon as he is home again.

She gave him a locket with her picture in it. Sometimes I see him looking at it for a long time. I know he misses her.

She must miss him, too. It must be hard to wait for somebody and not know if they are coming back. I miss my family and my friends.

At night, Captain Lewis and I sit together and stare up at the stars. It seems like we are just as far away from home as those stars are from us.

I guess I have been learning about myself, just like my parents said I would. Just the other day, I realized that I hadn't thought of running away in a long, long time.

Now the land looks different again. Steep cliffs rise up along the riverbanks. Strange animals live in the cliffs. They are sheep with big horns that curve behind their ears. These sheep look like they weigh about three hundred pounds. Still, they leap along these cliffs as if they could fly. I don't know how they do it. They never fall.

We have been seeing lots of porcupine. I know enough not to hunt them. I'm not going to end up with a nose full of needles!

June 2, 1805

The Missouri River and the Marias River, Montana

Today we came to a fork in the river. The water split off in two directions. Which one was still the Missouri? If we choose the wrong one, we'll lose valuable time.

The captains and crew studied the forks. The north was brown and muddy like the Missouri. The south fork looked like a clear mountain stream.

Most of the Corps thought we should go north. I knew they were wrong. So did Lewis and Clark.

The Hidatsa had told the captains about a great waterfall on the Missouri. It was in the mountains. The fork that looked like a mountain stream must be the right one.

But nobody else agreed with the captains, and even though I barked at them, nobody listened to me.

June 13, 1805

Searching for the Missouri

Captain Lewis decided to explore the south fork of the river. I went with him. He told me if he found the Great Falls, we knew it had to be the Missouri.

Today we found the Great Falls. One of them, at least.

What a beautiful sight it was! The river plunged over an 80-foot cliff. As the water crashed onto the rocks below, it sent up clouds of spray. The sound of the water roared in my ears. My tail wagged with excitement.

Captain Lewis's eyes sparkled. I think this was the grandest sight we have seen so far. I could have stood in that spot for days.

June 14, 1805

Heading up the Missouri

Today we found another waterfall. Then we found another and *another.*

Altogether, five of them make up the Great Falls. The Hidatsa had only mentioned one.

The Great Falls really did look great. But we couldn't go over them in boats. That meant we'd have to carry all our stuff around them. *That* isn't going to be great.

June 16, 1805

At the Great Falls

Today, when Captain Lewis and I got back to the camp from hunting, Captain Clark's face wore a worried look. He told us that Sacagawea was sick with a fever. She had stomach pains.

I ran to her tent, with Captain Lewis right behind me. Sacagawea was lying on a blanket. I tapped her with my paw and she opened her eyes. She smiled a little, then closed them again.

Captain Lewis gave Sacagawea water to drink from a nearby sulfur spring. He told her the water had healing powers. He gave her some bark tea, too.

I hope she will get better.

June 18, 1805

At the Great Falls

Sacagawea is getting stronger day by day. Meanwhile, the captains and I are caring for Pomp. We play with him, too.

Pomp likes to ride on my back while Captain Clark holds him. He laughs and makes noises. I think he is trying to say "bear."

June 22, 1805

Going around the Great Falls

The trip around the Great Falls began today. The men will move our six canoes in cottonwood wagons. They'll also move our other belongings to a new camp on the other side of the falls. The place is called White Bear Islands.

Captain Lewis has made me a special harness. When a rope is attached, I can help pull the wagons. I'm glad I can do my part.

Captain Lewis has brought along parts for an

iron boat. He invented it himself. He'll stay in the new camp at White Bear Islands and put it together.

June 26, 1805

Going around the Great Falls

Every day the men haul the heavy wagons around the falls. It takes every bit of strength they have.

Sometimes they roast in the heat. Other days bring storms of roaring wind, rain, and hailstones. They cut their feet on prickly pear cactus needles and rocks.

I know just how painful the prickly pear needles can be. I cut my feet on them, too. I only made one trip around the falls. Now I stay with Captain Lewis at White Bear Islands.

I would like to help the men with the carrying, but there are too many grizzly bears here around the new camp. Captain Lewis needs me to stand guard.

Sacagawea is all better. She and Pomp are staying at the new camp. Several of the men are, too.

The men are helping to clean and dry animal skins to cover the frame of Captain Lewis's boat.

Sacagawea and I watch them work. "I think the captain's heart will sink like his boat," she told me.

June 30, 1805

Going around the Great Falls

One day, Captain Clark went to look for some bundles that fell off a wagon. Charbonneau, Sacagawea, and I went with him. Sacagawea carried Pomp on her back.

By the time we reached the falls, storm clouds were gathering. Strong winds began to blow and hailstones pelted the ground. Soon, rain poured from the sky.

We found a ravine and huddled under a rock ledge. We could hear the hailstones thudding on the ground.

Water began pouring into the ravine. The rushing water pushed dirt and boulders down the hill. We were caught in a flash flood!

The ravine was filling up fast. It was almost up

to the captain's waist. I clawed my way out of the rocks.

Captain Clark lifted Sacagawea up toward me. I grabbed her robe in my mouth and pulled her up. Pomp was securely strapped to her back. Then I pulled Charbonneau up by his coat. Captain Clark climbed up by himself.

We ran through the rain and hail. On the way, we met up with York. He had been out hunting when the storm broke. Somehow we made it back to the camp. Pomp's cradleboard broke on the way, so York carried him in his arms.

"Good job, Sea," Captain Clark said when we were safe. "You kept calm, and you were a big help."

Maybe there is a little bit of hero in me after all. But I guess we're all heroes in the Corps of Discovery.

July 4, 1805

Beyond the Great Falls

It's Independence Day again! Tonight we will celebrate with dancing, but we need to go to sleep early.

We finished carrying everything around the

falls yesterday, so we need to rest up for the next part of the journey. We are waiting for Captain Lewis to finish the iron boat, too. I think it's got about as much chance of floating as a wagon full of rocks. I don't know how the captain got this idea into his head.

July 9, 1805

Heading up the Missouri again

Today we launched the iron boat. For a little while, it looked as if things would be okay. At first, the boat floated like a cork on the water. Then it sank like a stone.

Sacagawea was right. The captain's heart sank along with that boat. I could tell from the look on his face. All of our spirits sank, too.

We had lost time waiting for the boat to be finished. Now we would lose more. The men would have to build more canoes.

I licked Lewis's hand. He just kept staring at the water.

"Never mind," Captain Clark told him. "We'll get some canoes made. Then we'll go find the Shoshone."

CHAPTER 9

July 15 – August 26, 1805

When Seaman and the Corps of Discovery learned the truth about the Northwest Passage, they were surprised — but they kept on going.

July 15, 1805

Heading up the Missouri

Captain Clark found some cottonwood trees. The men made two more canoes. Now we are on our way again.

The Missouri looks different now. It isn't muddy anymore.

The journey has not gotten any easier. The current is still strong. The water tumbles over rocks and rushes around cliffs. The gnats and mosquitoes are still bad.

To the west we can see the Rockies. I thought

we'd find some small mountains. I wasn't expecting anything like these steep, jagged peaks.

July 19, 1805

Near the border of Idaho and Montana

The captains are in a hurry to find the Shoshone. Captain Clark and a few men have gone ahead to look for the tribe.

Our boats passed through the Gates of the Rocky Mountains. What a spooky place it was. Rocky cliffs towered above us on both sides. Giant boulders looked like they would tumble down and crush us at any minute.

But as soon as we passed through the canyon, we saw beautiful plains. Sacagawea is beginning to remember this land. She says the river will branch into three forks soon. Then her people, the Shoshone, will be near.

July 27, 1805

Three Forks, near the Idaho—Montana border

We arrived at the three forks in the river today. Then we made camp. Captain Clark came limping into camp this afternoon. He looked worn out.

His feet were bleeding from prickly pear needles and rocks. He had chills and fever. He had not seen any Shoshone.

Now Captain Lewis and Captain Clark say we'll head into one of the river's forks they have named the Jefferson, after the president. Soon we will have to cross over the Rocky Mountains. I hope we find the Shoshone soon and get horses.

July 28, 1805

On the Jefferson River

I have been wondering about Sacagawea. How did she end up in the Hidatsa village so far from her home?

Sometimes it's as if Sacagawea can read my thoughts. Today we were out walking, when she started talking to me. I guess the place had stirred up old memories.

About four years ago, she told me, a Hidatsa raiding party attacked her village. She and her friend Jumping Fish tried to hide in the woods. Hidatsa braves found them. She was kidnapped, but Jumping Fish got away.

Right now we are camped in the exact spot

where it happened. I don't know how she can stand it. Yet she is always calm. I think she is very brave.

She told me that while she was a captive of the Hidatsa, she met Charbonneau. He wanted her to be his wife. It was better than being a slave. If she hadn't married him, she wouldn't have little Pomp. And Pomp makes her so happy, she said.

I hadn't thought about it before, but now I know why Sacagawea and York understand each other so well. They don't speak the same language, but they both know what it is to be a slave.

August 8, 1805

On the Jefferson River

We are just about ready to collapse. The heat is terrible. Big blackflies have joined the gnats and mosquitoes in tormenting us.

We passed a big rock that looked like a beaver's head. Sacagawea remembered it. She said the Shoshone spend summers nearby.

That cheered everybody up a little.

Tomorrow, Lewis and I will go ahead to look for the Shoshone. We'll take Drouillard and two other men.

Captain Lewis asked Sacagawea how to say "white man." She wasn't sure. White men had not visited the Shoshone before.

Ta-ba-bone was the word she told him. It means "stranger."

August 12, 1805

On the Jefferson River

Today was a big day. Captain Lewis and our small band crossed the Continental Divide. Behind us, rivers flow east toward the Atlantic Ocean. Ahead, they flow west to the Pacific. As we climbed over a ridge, I could tell Lewis was excited. He said, "I expect to see a great plain to the west, with a large river flowing to the Pacific." I knew that this river would be the fabled Northwest Passage.

Well, we climbed over the ridge, and guess what we saw? The biggest, steepest, scariest mountains ever. (These were the Bitterroot Range of the Rocky Mountains. — Elvis)

If there is an easy coast-to-coast water route, this sure isn't it. Captain Lewis looks upset. It seems there is no Northwest Passage after all. But

Lewis tells us we have to keep going. He wants to reach the Pacific Ocean.

August 13, 1805

Headed for the Bitterroot Mountains

Today we met three Shoshone women. At first they seemed scared to death of us.

One was an old lady. Lewis took her hand. He pointed to his white skin and said *"Ta-ba-bone."*

Lewis painted the women's faces. He gave them presents of beads and mirrors. It made them all happy, and the old lady was happiest of all.

It was a good thing, too. A few minutes later, a Shoshone war party showed up.

There were about 60 warriors. They wore otter-skin cloaks. Some had otter-skin bands around their heads. There were eagle feathers in their hair and in their horses' manes.

Uh-oh, I thought. They sure don't look happy to see us. It's a good thing that old lady liked her gifts.

The old lady showed them her presents. She smiled and nodded. It got us off to a good start.

Then Captain Lewis put down his rifle and

picked up his flag. Pretty soon the chief came over. He said his name was Cameahwait. He put his left arm over the captain's shoulder.

The chief said, *"Ah-hi-e, ah-hi-e."* It means "I am much pleased." Then he looked at me and said the same words. Even though the men in the Corps didn't understand the chief, they sensed his greeting was friendly.

August 15, 1805

Camping with the Shoshone

I have been learning about the Shoshone. It is a sad story.

The Blackfeet, Hidatsa, and others raided their camps. They took their horses and destroyed their buffalo-skin lodges. Now they live in willow-brush huts.

With so many enemies around, it's hard for the Shoshone to hunt. They have only bows and arrows and no guns. They are poor, and they are thin. The people are still very cheerful, though.

August 16, 1805

Camping with the Shoshone

Captain Lewis asked Cameahwait how to get to the Columbia River. The chief said we have to cross the Bitterroot Mountains, which are a very steep and rugged range of the Rocky Mountains. He warned that it was a terrible journey.

One of the Shoshone men, Old Toby, has crossed the mountains before with the Nez Percé. Every year they go over the Lolo trail to hunt buffalo.

Captain Lewis says if the Nez Percé can do it, so can we. It sounds frightening, but I'm ready for the challenge.

August 17, 1805

Camping with the Shoshone

Two incredible things happened to Sacagawea today.

When Sacagawea, Captain Clark, and the others walked into the camp, a Shoshone woman ran to Sacagawea and hugged her. It was Jumping Fish, her childhood friend. They thought they would never see each other again.

Then everyone sat down for a meeting to discuss buying horses. Sacagawea began to interpret. The words went through a chain. The Shoshone spoke to Sacagawea. Then she spoke to Charbonneau in Hidatsa. Charbonneau spoke to Francois LaBiche, a member of the Corps, in French. LaBiche spoke to the captains in English. That is how the Shoshone words finally reached Lewis and Clark.

All of a sudden, Sacagawea got very quiet. She stared at Cameahwait and started to cry. Then she ran over and hugged him.

It turned out the chief was her brother!

This miracle was lucky for us. Cameahwait agreed to sell us all the horses we wanted.

It is no wonder that Lewis and Clark have decided to name this spot Camp Fortunate.

August 26, 1805

Camping with the Shoshone

We will soon leave the Shoshone. Sacagawea has been so happy here, I thought that she might decide to stay with her people. While we were walking at night, she said to me: "Bear-Dog, I have come this far. Now I want to see the great ocean." She said she knew crossing the mountains would be hard. But she was not afraid. And now, neither am I.

CHAPTER 10
September 1–
October 4, 1805

The Corps faced their biggest challenge when they climbed the Bitterroot Mountains. Would they survive?

September 1, 1805

Heading for the Bitterroot Mountains

We are on our way to the Bitterroot Mountains. I know we have seen tough times before. I think we are in for the toughest yet. But, strangely, I am ready.

September 9, 1805

On the Idaho–Montana border

We are camped out. The captains call this place Travelers Rest.

We sure need rest and plenty of it. The horses are

already tired. I am weak with hunger. All we have to eat now is salt pork.

At first I thought our guide was old and frail. But Old Toby is as tough as they come. It's a good thing, too. He is the only one who knows the way over the mountains.

September 11, 1805

Crossing the Bitterroot Mountains

We are on our way again. Now we will actually climb the mountains. Yesterday I caught a few pheasants. I just grabbed them in my mouth one by one and brought them to camp.

It's a good thing the pheasants were slow. I don't know how much longer I will be able to hunt. If I don't get more food soon, I will be too weak.

September 14, 1805

Crossing the Bitterroot Mountains

It rained, hailed, and snowed today. Old Toby got lost.

We tried to hunt but found no game. One of the colts died. We were all so hungry that we ate it.

September 15, 1805

Crossing the Bitterroot Mountains

Old Toby found his way again. Even so, we almost didn't make it back to the trail. The ground was covered with fallen trees.

Captain Clark always cheers us on, no matter what. "Come on, you can do it!" he says.

Captain Lewis doesn't say much. He just keeps going and never complains. It seems that he could go on forever.

September 17, 1805

Crossing the Bitterroot Mountains

It's been snowing all day long. We are all cold, wet, and starving.

This is the worst time of the entire expedition. Yesterday we were so hungry we ate our candles. I'll never forget that gluey, waxy taste.

This is the worst. I am almost too weak to write.

September 25, 1805

Washington State

Somehow we made it out of the Bitterroot Mountains.

Now we are in the village of the Nez Percé. Chief Twisted Hair and his people are very friendly. They gave us their food to eat.

We all chowed down on the salmon and camas root. The men said it made them as sick as dogs. I still don't understand that expression.

September 26, 1805

Camping with the Nez Percé

The Nez Percé live in lodges made of wooden poles covered with reed mats. They are big enough for several families.

Their clothes are made of deer and antelope hide. Men wear pants and jackets with fringed sleeves and headbands of otter fur. The chiefs wear headdresses with lots of feathers.

Women wear long dresses and knee-high moccasins. They decorate their clothes with elk teeth and shells.

Some of the Nez Percé wear jewelry made of shells in their noses. Nez Percé means "pierced noses."

September 27, 1805

Camping with the Nez Percé

The Corps is still sick from the food. But they have started making canoes.

Chief Twisted Hair showed them the Nez Percé method. They put the logs over a fire to hollow out the inside. It looks a lot easier than chopping out the logs with axes.

Today I met a woman named Watkuweis. It means "Returned from a Far Country." She and Sacagawea talked for a long time. I listened.

One day about six years ago, Watkuweis was kidnapped by the Blackfeet. They sold her to a white trader.

"I lived among the whites for years. They were kind to me," she said. "But one day I left them. I found my way back to my people."

Watkuweis never forgot how the whites helped her. That is why she helped the Corps. When we first arrived, sick and weak, some had talked of killing us. They wanted our guns and other things. We might have been murdered, and we never even knew it.

Watkuweis made them stop such talk. She reminded them that the whites had treated her well. "Do them no hurt," she said.

Sacagawea told Watkuweis about her own kidnapping. I'm glad she has found someone to share her sorrows with.

I like it here with the Nez Percé. Salmon tastes pretty good to me, especially when I don't have to fish for it.

Tomorrow the canoes will be finished. I will travel to the Pacific Ocean with Captain Lewis and Captain Clark. I am sorry to leave the Nez Percé, but I can't wait to see the ocean. I'm a water dog, after all.

October 7, 1805

Heading into the Clearwater River, Idaho

We launched the canoes into the Clearwater River. It leads to the Snake River, and then the Columbia. Chief Twisted Hair will come with us part of the way.

October 14, 1805

On the Snake River

We have made it through some very rough rapids. Our canoes flipped over and rammed against the rocks. It was the last straw for Old Toby.

The Bitterroot Mountains did not scare him, but the rapids did. Last night he ran away.

CHAPTER 11
October 18, 1805 – March 23, 1806

The Corps met new tribes and had more adventures. All the while Seaman wondered if they would ever reach the ocean.

October 18, 1805

On the Columbia River, at the Oregon–Washington border

Two days ago, we reached the Columbia River. All along the riverbanks people are catching salmon. One night we were invited to dinner. A man cooked salmon in a basket filled with hot stones and water. It was the best salmon I ever ate.

Captain Clark liked it almost as much as I did. He gave the man some ribbons. That made him pretty happy.

October 24, 1805

On the Columbia River

We have entered Chinook country. Twisted Hair went back to his village. He told us the Chinook were at war with the Nez Percé.

I think we are passing through the worst rapids ever. But we have no choice but to stay in the boat. It is impossible to carry our things over land. There are rocky ledges on both sides of the river.

The natives are experts with canoes. I know they don't think we will make it. Hundreds gather on the riverbanks to watch us drown. We'll show them. The Corps is used to doing the impossible. And with a Newfoundland like me on their team, there's no way they can drown.

November 3, 1805

On the Columbia River

We made it through the rapids. "The Corps has done it again, Seaman," said Captain Lewis. Then he pointed to the sea otters we were passing in the river. "Sea otters mean that the ocean is near."

The little fellows had long, glossy fur, long bodies, and short legs. They were diving and floating in the water. I think they would be fun to play with. They even have webbed feet like me!

It looks like we have entered a new land. Forests of spruce, fir, pine, and cedar are all around us. The weather is different, too. Now there is rain and fog, fog and rain.

Villages of the Chinook tribe dot the riverbanks. They look different from any other people I have ever seen before.

The Chinook think that flat heads with pointed tops look good. They get them that way by fastening boards on their babies' heads. It flattens them little by little, and it doesn't hurt.

The Chinook are wonderful canoe makers. They make 50-foot-long boats decorated with beautiful carvings. You'd think it would take a year to make one, but it only takes the Chinook a few weeks.

While we waited for the canoes, I swam with the otters. It was fun to play with animals again, but I sure miss Marcel.

November 7, 1805

On the Columbia River

Today I noticed that the air smelled different. Salty. I could feel salt on my fur. I lapped up some of the water and it tasted salty, too. I looked up and saw a seagull.

Suddenly, Captain Clark got very quiet. "Listen!" he said. "I can hear waves breaking on rocks."

Everyone began to cheer. I howled with joy and wagged my tail. At last we had reached the Pacific Ocean.

Tonight when everyone was asleep, I peeked at Captain Clark's journal. Today's entry was, "Ocian in view! O! the joy." (He meant "ocean," of course.)

November 10, 1805

The Columbia River Estuary

False alarm. We have not reached the ocean after all. We were in something called an estuary. That is where the river current mixes with the ocean tides. The water was salty because the river current and the ocean tides were mixing.

The ocean is nearby, but we are going to have to wait awhile to see it. Bad storms and high winds make it impossible for us to go anywhere. We're stuck.

We have made a camp on some rocky ground. Every day we are battered by thunder and lightning and rain. Sometimes the wind is so fierce that trees come crashing down. We'll be stuck here for a while.

November 18, 1805

The Pacific Ocean, at the
Oregon–Washington border

At last we were able to travel 20 more miles. Then we finally saw the great Pacific Ocean. Everyone was very quiet. We just stood there on the beach and stared at the waves. We had traveled for 18 months to get here. It was a truly amazing sight. My tail thumped when I saw all that blue water. I love an ocean view — all Newfoundlands do.

We have moved our camp downriver. Tonight some Chinook came to visit with two of their chiefs.

One of the chiefs had a beautiful robe made of sea

otter skins. Captain Lewis wanted that robe, but the chief wouldn't part with it. He turned down everything the captain offered to trade.

Then Sacagawea took off her belt. It was made of beautiful blue beads. She held it out to the chief. A big, wide grin spread over his face as he took it in his hands. He turned the belt over and over, examining the blue beads.

Now the chief handed the otter skin coat to Sacagawea. She passed it right to Captain Lewis.

The captain didn't say anything for a few moments. He just held the coat and looked at Sacagawea.

"Janey, that was very kind of you," he said finally. I could tell that he thought she had done something very special. Then Captain Lewis gave Sacagawea his own blue coat.

November 22, 1805

Oregon–Washington border

We were visited by some people from the Clatsop tribe. They come from the other side of the river. They told us there are plenty of elk to hunt there.

November 24, 1805

Oregon

Today was a big day. We decided where to make our winter quarters.

There were two choices. We could stay on the north side of the river with the Chinook. Or we could stay on the south side with the Clatsop.

To me it was a no-brainer. The Clatsop were friendlier. There was more game on the south side. Plus, we'd be closer to the ocean.

The captains could have easily told everyone where to stay. Instead, they took a vote. Nobody was left out, including York and Sacagawea. (Neither slaves nor Native Americans nor women had the right to vote in the U.S. at that time. So it was special that the captains included them. — Elvis)

We will stay with the Clatsop.

December 7, 1805

Camping with the Clatsop

We have started building Fort Clatsop, our winter quarters.

It rains, and rains, and rains. My fur never seems to get dry.

The Clatsop weren't kidding about the elk. There are plenty of them around. Elk is all we ever eat, day after day after day.

December 23, 1805

Camping with the Clatsop

We moved into our lodges even though the roofs aren't finished. The fleas moved in, too. We just can't get rid of them! I'm very itchy.

December 25, 1805

Camping with the Clatsop

Merry Christmas! This morning the men sang songs. After breakfast, the captains gave out hand-kerchiefs as presents. Captain Lewis even tied one around my neck. We all were cheerful.

It hardly ever stops raining here. Clothes and blankets never get dry.

Meat rots fast in this damp climate. Today we ate spoiled elk. It smelled pretty bad. It's a little bit sad to be having Christmas so far from home.

December 29, 1805

Camping with the Clatsop

Today something exciting happened. The Clatsop told us a whale had washed ashore. Captain Clark is getting together a party to go and bring back meat.

Sacagawea asked to go along. Captain Clark said no.

It wasn't fair. I started to growl.

"Don't you two gang up on me," said Captain Clark. "It isn't safe. We'll travel by canoe over rough water, and Janey and Pomp might get sick."

I had never gotten angry with Clark before, but what he said made no sense at all. Sacagawea and Pomp had done as much rough traveling as everyone else, and she should have been allowed to see the big fish.

I growled again. Sacagawea looked angry enough to growl, too. Instead she said just what I had been thinking.

Lewis had been quiet. Now he spoke up. "I think Sacagawea should go," he told Clark.

Clark thought for a minute. "You're right," he said. "So are Seaman and Sacagawea."

Sacagawea threw her arms around my neck. She thanked me for being on her side.

January 8, 1806

Camping with the Clatsop

On our way to the beach we saw 14 women with baskets of blubber (whale fat). Plenty of others had gotten to the whale before we did. It was a 105-foot-long skeleton and a pretty amazing sight.

Sacagawea walked around the skeleton again and again. Pomp toddled over and peeked inside. I looked in, too. It was like staring into a cave made of bones.

Later, Captain Clark bought 300 pounds of whale blubber from the Clatsop. The meat was kind of chewy, but anything is better than more elk.

February 22, 1806

Camping with the Clatsop

Almost all the men have colds. Our quarters are cold, damp, and smoky. We never got rid of the fleas. The men are making lots of moccasins. They are starting to get ready for the trip home. I'm ready, too.

March 23, 1806

Leaving Fort Clatsop

Today we left Fort Clatsop. It rained all but 12 days while we were there. I am looking forward to feeling clean and dry. I can't wait to get rid of these fleas. Soon we will be back with the Nez Percé. *Whew!*

CHAPTER 12
May 11–
Thanksgiving Day, 1806

Seaman traveled a great distance, and learned that he was not the same dog who never wanted to leave the Pittsburgh wharves.

May 11, 1806

Camping with the Nez Percé

We are in the Nez Percé village again. The Corps is getting more and more restless. They want to get started across the Bitterroot Mountains. They want to go home, but Chief Twisted Hair says the snow is still too deep. We have to wait for it to melt. Every day the men mope around. Sometimes they have footraces with the Nez Percé. The fastest runners in the Corps are

Reuben Field and George Drouillard. They hardly ever lose.

I don't want to cross the Bitterroot Mountains again. But I am so eager to see my family and tell them about my travels.

June 10, 1806

Back on the Columbia River

This morning we said good-bye to the Nez Percé. We are going home! I can't believe how different I feel from when we started the trip. Now the wilderness doesn't seem as scary to me. I know I did it once, so I know I can do it again.

September 23, 1806

St. Louis, Missouri

So much time has gone by. I haven't had a chance to write because we've been busy speeding our way back East. We covered more than 70 miles a day and sometimes didn't even stop to hunt! It was rough going at times, but we all made it back in one piece. The saddest day of the trip was probably August 14, when we arrived back at the

Mandan villages and had to say good-bye to Sacagawea and Pomp. They would be returning to their
home with Charbonneau. Sacagawea scratched me
behind the ears and whispered a special good-bye
to me. I licked her face in return. I hope she understood what I couldn't say in words: that we
couldn't have made it through the expedition without her — and that I will never forget her.

Now we are in St. Louis, Missouri. The Corps
is going to split up and return to their homes and
families. But Lewis and Clark have been invited to
Washington, D.C., to attend special parties and see
the president. Lewis told Clark he will be bringing
me along!

Thanksgiving Day, 1806

The Pittsburgh wharves

Again, I haven't had any time to write in my
journal. The past few months have been so busy.
But the important thing is that I'm now back home
with my friends and family. I'll have to sum up all
that has happened after the expedition ended.

Earlier in the fall, I went with Lewis and Clark
to Washington. Everybody was so excited to see

them. They were heroes! Big parties were held in their honor. I overheard one man in Washington tell Lewis it was as if they had just returned from the moon! It did feel that way.

I wasn't allowed to attend all the parties (I don't understand why people are reluctant to let dogs into fancy places. We know how to behave ourselves!), but I did get to go to the White House! I was thrilled to meet President Jefferson. He is so proud of Lewis and Clark, and he gave me a pat on the head and said he was proud of me, too. I hope he didn't notice me blushing under my fur.

Lewis and Clark had discovered there was no Northwest Passage and reported this to President Jefferson. This fact disappointed the president, but he was happy about the new information they had brought back with them. The expedition had discovered 178 new species of animals (that's including prairie dogs, of course!) and 122 new species of plants. They wrote about the language and culture of more than 50 Native American tribes. Twenty-two of those tribes had never before seen a white man.

The captains also took me to visit the president

at his home in Virginia. It was a big and beautiful house they called Monticello. Guess who I saw there? Marcel! He was outside waiting for me, chattering away happily. He said he was having a really good time living on the grounds of Monticello.

He told me there were other prairie dogs on the grounds. "We tunnel and make burrows!" he said.

"We sure had some great adventures together, didn't we?" I asked.

Marcel said it was true. We did have some amazing times. It was great to talk about old times with my old friend.

Finally, Lewis and Clark brought me back to the Pittsburgh wharves. The captains thanked me for being so courageous on the trip. They said I'd been a true hero the whole time. I barked happily back at them. Little did they know what a scaredy-dog I'd been when the trip began. *They* had really made a hero out of *me*!

My family and friends were even happier to see me than I'd imagined. My parents couldn't stop looking at me and grinning.

"I can't put my paw on it, but you're different," my mom told me.

My dad nodded. "You seem wiser," he said.

I told my parents how I had grown to love traveling and adventure. I told them everything I had seen and done.

"You're a hero, Seaman," Mom said.

"I'm proud of you," Dad told me.

Just three years ago, if someone had told me I'd one day be called a hero, I would have howled with laughter. But I've changed so much. I know now what the world beyond Pittsburgh holds. It's filled with many dangers but also many wonders. The expedition has taught me an important lesson: The unknown will always seem scary. But you have to take a chance sometimes and go out into new places so you can learn more about yourself and the world around you.

I definitely have a lot to be grateful for today. I'm thankful for having the opportunity to go on the Lewis and Clark expedition, I'm thankful that I had the strength to survive it, and now I'm thankful to be back home. Maybe someday I will travel again, but for now, it is nice to rest, relax, swim, and eat with my friends and family.

Epilogue
by Elvis

Captain Clark continued to have good luck. He was successful as governor of the Missouri Territory. However, Captain Lewis was not so lucky. He never married. His early success soon disappeared. He fell into debt and became unhappy. Captain Lewis died in 1809. Some say he was murdered by robbers. Others think he took his own life. I don't know for sure.

Sacagawea and Captain Clark remained friends. One day she and her husband took Pomp to live with him. Clark made sure Pomp got an education. He grew up to become a guide to the West. Clark died in St. Louis in 1838. His funeral was one of the most impressive that the city's residents had ever seen.

Most historians say Sacagawea died in 1812. Some believe she lived until 1884 and died among the Shoshone.

Members of the Corps of Discovery

I'm sure Seaman wishes he could have written about each and every member of the Corps of Discovery. However, he probably didn't have time. Plus, it's hard to write in secret. Seaman had to borrow the paper, pen, and ink from Captain Lewis, without him knowing, and write by candlelight. Now that I have more time, I'd like to give this list of all the members of the Lewis and Clark expedition:

Meriwether Lewis and William Clark
William Bratton
Toussaint Charbonneau
Jean-Baptiste Charbonneau ("Pomp")
John Collins
John Colter
Pierre Cruzatte
Pierre Dorion
George Drouillard
Joseph Field
Reuben Field
Charles Floyd
Robert Frazer
Patrick Gass

George Gibson

Silas Goodrich

Hugh Hall

Thomas P. Howard

Francois LaBiche

Jean Baptiste LePage

Hugh McNeal

John Newman (dismissed)

John Ordway

John Potts

Nathaniel Pryor

Moses Reed (dismissed)

George Shannon

John Shields

John B. Thompson

Richard Warfington

Peter Weiser

William Werner

Joseph Whitehouse

Alexander Willard

Richard Windsor

Sacagawea

York (Clark's slave)

Native American Tribes

Seaman encountered more than 50 Native American tribes with Lewis and Clark. The ones listed below are the ones they got to know best. Seaman wrote about almost all of them in his journal.

Arikara

Assinboin

Chinook

Clatsop

Hidatsa

Mandan

Missouri

Nez Percé

Otoe

Shoshone

Teton Sioux

Tilamook

Walla Walla

Wishram

Yankton Sioux

Stuff I Learned About Newfoundlands

Newfoundlands are water dogs. Their thick coats keep them warm, and repel water. They have webbed feet.

The Newfoundland breed was developed on the coast of (guess where?) Newfoundland. The year was around 1700.

Newfoundlands often worked on fishing boats. They hauled nets and pulled carts. They also pulled drowning sailors from the water.

Many Newfoundlands have black coats like Seaman did. Some of them are brown. The breed's weight is usually 99 to 150 pounds.

MORE SERIES YOU'LL LOVE

A Jigsaw Jones Mystery™

Jigsaw and his partner, Mila, know that mysteries are like jigsaw puzzles—you've got to look at all the pieces to solve the case!

THE SECRETS OF DROON

Under the stairs a magical world awaits you.

Hey L'il D!

L'il Dobber has two things with him at all times—his basketball and his friends. Together, they are a great team. And they are always looking for adventure and fun—on and off the b'ball court!

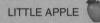